HOW DO FAIRIES HAVE FUN IN THE SUN?

Liza Gardner Walsh

Illustrated by Hazel Mitchell

Down East Books

Camden, Maine
Guilford, Connecticut

To my nephews, William and Bennett,
who are always open to adventure.
—L. G. W.

To L.G.W., who loves summer.
—H. M.

Down East Books

An imprint of The Rowman & Littlefield Publishing Group, Inc.
4501 Forbes Blvd., Ste. 200
Lanham, MD 20706

Distributed by National Book Network

British Library Cataloguing-in-Publication Information available

Library of Congress Control Number: 2017961279

ISBN 978-1-60893-993-0 (hardcover)
ISBN 978-1-60893-994-7 (e-book)

♾™ The paper used in this publication meets the minimum requirements of American National Standard for Information Sciences—Permanence of Paper for Printed Library Materials,
ANSI/NISO Z39.48-1992.

MOST people know fairies
love the summer sun,
But how do they soak up
all of its endless fun?

CMANY say that summer's the fairies favorite season,
But why do YOU think, what are the reasons?

BEFORE the day begins, do they slather on sunscreen,
Then fill up their lunch boxes and water canteens?

DO they wear miniature sunglasses to protect their eyes
As they sit on the beach to watch the sunrise?

CAN their wings get wet? Can they swim in the pool?

Or do they just dip toes in to keep themselves cool?

Maybe they prefer to careen through the waves,

Riding birch bark boards while soaking up rays?

OR do they don life jackets
and head out for a sail,
Their fairy boats bobbing
amidst wind and whales?

Do they put on shorts and hiking boots,

To climb up mountains along woodsy routes?

Do they set up bake sales
and nectar stands,
To raise money for all
of their giant plans?

BAKE SALE

AFTERWARD do they sit in tiny rocking chairs,
Sipping their nectar and planning elaborate fairs?

DO they construct
roller coasters
and water slides,
So the fairy children
can take wild rides?

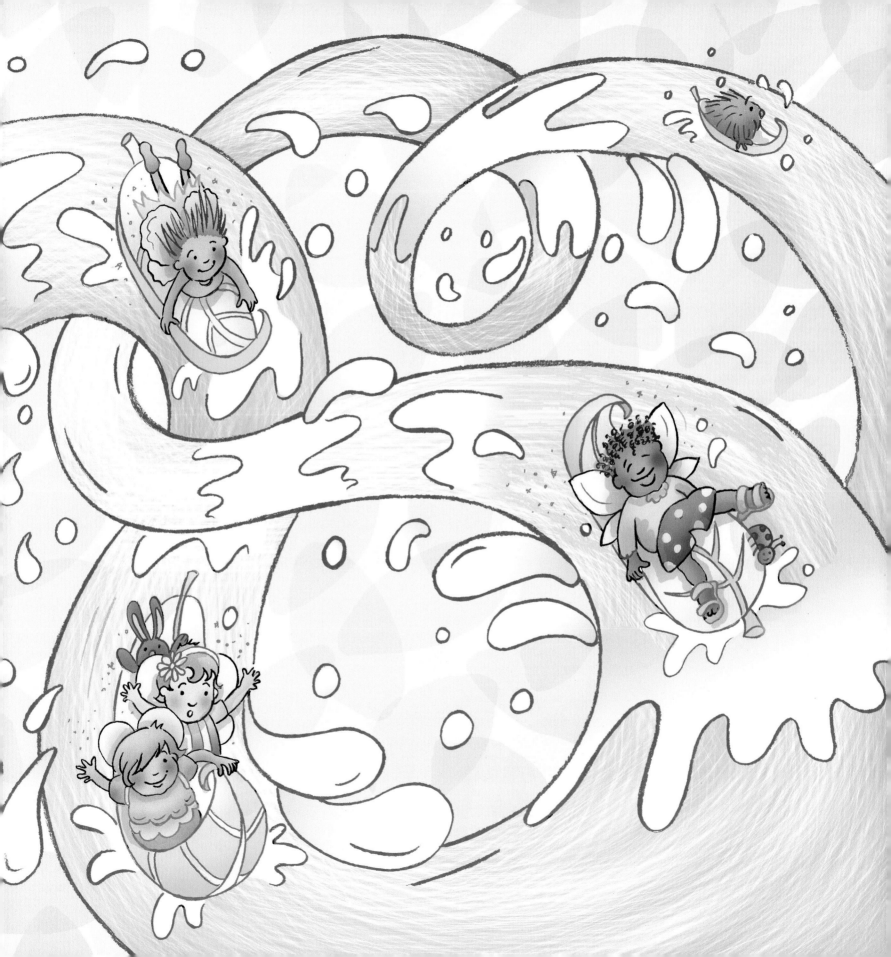

PERHAPS all this activity
is a bit too extreme,
For the fairies do love
napping, it seems.

MAYBE they just eat ice cream, popsicles, and berries,
And simply watch as YOU assemble houses for fairies.

PERHAPS they marvel
at each treasure you find,
Amazed that you take
so much time to be kind.

And when you finish each tiny house in the woods,
Do the fairies climb in to check out all the goods?

Do they rest in the little beds that you carefully made,
Closing their eyes, letting the summer light fade?

Perhaps it's a mix of naps and busy play
That keeps summer fairies exploring each day?

FOR exploring is the trademark of this bountiful time,
So get outside, look around, enjoy nature in its prime.

For that is the ultimate wish of the fairies all year,
No matter the season, they hope you hold nature dear.

How To Build A Fairy House

STEP 1: Find a good spot. Fairies need plenty of privacy and protection from wind, dogs, and big feet. Some good sites are tree hollows, tree roots or uprooted trees, stone walls, beaches, stumps, and flower gardens.

STEP 2: Gather your supplies. Most important, make sure you have a good pile of bark to form your walls.

STEP 3: Start to build. You can lean bark or sticks up against a tree or rock to make a lean-to. You can balance bark in an A shape. Or you might find a perfect hollow in a tree and not need to build walls at all.

STEP 4: Think about furniture next. Fairies need a bed to take naps in, but what else do you want in there?

STEP 5: Now step back and look at the entrance to your house. Can you make a pathway of tiny pinecones? Or a sea glass and seashell patio? Do you have a fairy door? Last of all, make sure you tidy up. Fairies are extraordinarily neat, and when they see that you have cleaned up all the extra debris, their hearts will sing with joy!

STEP 6: Continue to watch your house and fix it up after it rains and the wind blows. Check for signs that fairies have visited.